Published by Ladybird Books Ltd
27 Wrights Lane London W8 5TZ
A Penguin Company
3 5 7 9 10 8 6 4 2

Printed in Italy

DISNEY'S
THE
LION KING II
SIMBA'S·PRIDE

Ladybird

The news swept like the wind across the Pride Lands. The animals gathered quickly at the foot of Pride Rock.

High on the ridge stood Simba the Lion King, Nala the Queen, Timon, Pumbaa and Rafiki.

Everyone watched as Rafiki gently lifted a tiny lion cub towards the skies.

"It's a girl! Welcome, Princess Kiara!" he cried.

Simba and Nala gave a big smile, and all the animals cheered. The Circle of Life was complete once more.

Rafiki knew that the birth of a princess would give the pride hope for the future, but that evening he was worried. He learnt that trouble was coming to the Pride Lands.

On the edge of the kingdom, a lioness
angrily grasped her cub. The lioness's
name was Zira. She had been the mate
of Scar, Simba's rival, and she blamed
Simba for Scar's death.

Banished from the pride, she now led
a group of rebels called the Outlanders.

Her two young spies, Nuka and Vitani,
returned with news of Kiara's birth.

"Perfect!" snarled Zira. A girl could not be king, but her son Kovu could. She gripped the little cub in her paws. He *would* take Simba's place.

Summer came swiftly to the Pride Lands. It was time for Kiara to go exploring. Pumbaa and Timon tried to keep an eye on her, but she soon left them behind. She scampered happily towards the river, and bounced from rock to rock… until she came face to face with Kovu. Kiara was pleased to meet a new friend.

Suddenly the rocks moved beneath them. The cubs were standing on crocodiles! Leaping in between the snapping jaws, Kiara and Kovu raced to the river bank.

The two cubs wanted to play together, but Simba and Zira arrived. They glared angrily at each other. It was time for Kovu and Kiara to say goodbye.

Simba warned Kiara to be more careful. "You're going to be queen one day," he told her. "It's part of who you are. We are all one in the Circle of Life."

Kovu was in trouble too. Zira told him to keep away from Kiara. "I'm sorry," said Kovu. "I thought we could be friends."

"Friends?" hissed Zira. But then she had an idea. If Kovu were to be accepted into the pride, then he would have a better chance to destroy Simba.

Seasons passed and Kovu grew into a strong young lion, ready to carry out his mother's evil plans.

And Kiara, now a beautiful lioness, was about to set out on her first hunt alone. "Daddy, you must promise to let me do this on my own," she told Simba. But the Lion King couldn't keep his promise. Secretly, he asked Timon and Pumbaa to go after her.

Kiara was furious when she found them. She raced away towards the grasslands.

But the princess didn't know that Zira's spies were following her. She was running straight into the Outlanders' trap. "Let's light the fires!" laughed Nuka and Vitani.

When Kiara noticed the flames around her, it was too late to escape. But Kovu appeared and bravely dragged the princess away to safety.

Kiara woke up suddenly and leapt to her feet. At first she didn't know the lion in front of her, but then she recognised him.

"Kovu?" she asked.

Simba, Nala and Rafiki arrived. They had seen the fires from Pride Rock and had run to the rescue.

They were glad that Kiara was safe. But they were not pleased to see Kovu, even though he had saved her life.

Kovu slowly approached Simba.
"I humbly ask to join your pride," he said.
So Simba decided to give the young
Outlander a chance. But the Lion King
would not let Kovu inside their cave at
Pride Rock.

The next morning Kiara asked Kovu to teach her how to hunt. "Relax," said Kovu. "Feel the earth under your paws."

He led her through the long grass and over a hill towards a flock of birds. There they startled Timon and Pumbaa who were searching for bugs.

Kiara and the others raced down the hill, scattering the birds. But they ran straight into a herd of rhinos.

"This way!" cried Kiara, and she led them to a cave until the danger had passed. Kiara and Kovu enjoyed their adventures that day. And at night-time they watched the stars together.

Looking up at the sky, Kiara began to talk about her father and grandfather. As she did so, Kovu came to doubt everything Zira had taught him.

Rafiki appeared in the shadows. "Follow me," he whispered, "to a special place in your heart. It is called Upendi."

They did. And when Kovu returned to Pride Rock with Kiara, he knew they would always be together. He could never go back to the Outlanders.

From a safe distance, Vitani watched Kovu near the Lion King's cave. Quickly she ran back to the Outlands to report to Zira that Kovu had left them.

Next morning the Outlanders set a trap for the Lion King in the ravine. But Simba managed to escape and, in the struggle, Nuka was crushed under some logs.

In grief and anger Zira struck Kovu, giving him a wound over his eye just like the one Scar had once had. Kovu went sadly back to Pride Rock.

But the Pridelanders drove him away, blaming Kovu for Zira's trap.

Kiara was the only one who still trusted Kovu and she followed him to a waterhole. He was overjoyed to see her again.

"We must go back," said Kiara. "If we run away, the pride will be divided for ever."

Meanwhile Zira had called her lionesses to war. As storm clouds gathered overhead, she led them into battle against the Pridelanders.

Kiara returned with Kovu just in time to beg for peace. Simba and all the animals knew that she was right. The division of the pride was not part of the Circle of Life.

Only Zira was determined to fight, and she tried to attack Simba. But Kiara came between them. As the two lionesses struggled, they reached the edge of the gorge. Zira slipped over the ridge – never to be seen again.

Simba declared peace across the Pride Lands. And a few days later, the whole pride gathered in a circle on the rocks. Kiara and Kovu came in last to complete the ring, and Rafiki gave them his blessing.

The Circle of Life was complete again and the pride could live happily together once more.

The Little Mermaid

First published in 2006 by
Franklin Watts
338 Euston Road
London
NW1 3BH

Franklin Watts Australia
Hachette Children's Books
Level 17/207 Kent Street
Sydney
NSW 2000

A CIP catalogue record for this book is available
from the British Library.

ISBN 0 7496 6577 7 (hbk)
ISBN 0 7496 6583 1 (pbk)

Series Editor: Jackie Hamley
Series Advisor: Dr Barrie Wade
Series Designer: Peter Scoulding

Printed in China

For Katy – my own Little Mermaid – A.A.

The Little Mermaid

Retold by Anne Adeney

Illustrated by Natascia Ugliano

FRANKLIN WATTS
LONDON•SYDNEY

Maren was a mermaid princess with a lovely voice.

She lived with her family beneath the sea.

Maren longed to see the world above the surface of the sea, but she was still too young.

6

7

On her fifteenth birthday, Maren was allowed to go to the surface like her older sisters.

"It's so beautiful,"
she thought.

Then Maren saw a ship.
Prince Gustav was having
a party on board.

Suddenly, there was a
big storm and the ship
quickly sank.

Maren rescued the handsome prince and left him on the beach.

12

The prince thought another girl had rescued him. "If only *I* had legs instead of a tail, I could be with the prince," said Maren.

Maren swam home, deep in the sea. She asked Runa, the witch, for a magic potion to give her legs.

Then she would be able to live with the prince above the surface.

"I will give you a potion, but you must pay," Runa warned. "You will lose your voice.

"Your new legs will always hurt you. And if your prince does not marry you, then you will die!"

Maren drank the potion and swam quickly to the surface.

Prince Gustav found her on the beach. She had legs now, but she could not talk or sing.

Maren was taken to
Prince Gustav's palace.

She was so happy, although
her legs hurt her terribly.

Gustav soon fell in love with her. "I love you, but I've promised to marry the girl who rescued me from the shipwreck," he said.

23

Next day, Gustav got
married, but not to Maren.

After the wedding, Maren's
sisters came to visit her.

"We gave Runa our hair for a spell to save your life," they said. "If you kill Gustav, you will not die!"

27

But Maren could
not kill him.

She dived into the sea and
melted into the waves.

Then Maren felt herself
lifted up into the air.
"We are the spirits of the
air," said the magical spirits.

"You have shown great
love, so you will never die.
And you can live in the
sky with us forever!"

Leapfrog has been specially designed to fit the requirements of the National Literacy Strategy. It offers real books for beginning readers by top authors and illustrators.

There are 49 Leapfrog stories to choose from:

The Bossy Cockerel
ISBN 0 7496 3828 1

Bill's Baggy Trousers
ISBN 0 7496 3829 X

Mr Spotty's Potty
ISBN 0 7496 3831 1

Little Joe's Big Race
ISBN 0 7496 3832 X

The Little Star
ISBN 0 7496 3833 8

The Cheeky Monkey
ISBN 0 7496 3830 3

Selfish Sophie
ISBN 0 7496 4385 4

Recycled!
ISBN 0 7496 4388 9

Felix on the Move
ISBN 0 7496 4387 0

Pippa and Poppa
ISBN 0 7496 4386 2

Jack's Party
ISBN 0 7496 4389 7

The Best Snowman
ISBN 0 7496 4390 0

Eight Enormous Elephants
ISBN 0 7496 4634 9

Mary and the Fairy
ISBN 0 7496 4633 0

The Crying Princess
ISBN 0 7496 4632 2

Jasper and Jess
ISBN 0 7496 4081 2

The Lazy Scarecrow
ISBN 0 7496 4082 0

The Naughty Puppy
ISBN 0 7496 4383 8

Freddie's Fears
ISBN 0 7496 4382 X

FAIRY TALES
Cinderella
ISBN 0 7496 4228 9

The Three Little Pigs
ISBN 0 7496 4227 0

Jack and the Beanstalk
ISBN 0 7496 4229 7

The Three Billy Goats Gruff
ISBN 0 7496 4226 2

Goldilocks and the Three Bears
ISBN 0 7496 4225 4

Little Red Riding Hood
ISBN 0 7496 4224 6

Rapunzel
ISBN 0 7496 6159 3

Snow White
ISBN 0 7496 6161 5

The Emperor's New Clothes
ISBN 0 7496 6163 1

The Pied Piper of Hamelin
ISBN 0 7496 6164 X

Hansel and Gretel
ISBN 0 7496 6162 3

The Sleeping Beauty
ISBN 0 7496 6160 7

Rumpelstiltskin
ISBN 0 7496 6165 8

The Ugly Duckling
ISBN 0 7496 6166 6

Puss in Boots
ISBN 0 7496 6167 4

The Frog Prince
ISBN 0 7496 6168 2

The Princess and the Pea
ISBN 0 7496 6169 0

Dick Whittington
ISBN 0 7496 6170 4

The Elves and the Shoemaker
ISBN 0 7496 6575 0*
ISBN 0 7496 6581 5

The Little Match Girl
ISBN 0 7496 6576 9*
ISBN 0 7496 6582 3

The Little Mermaid
ISBN 0 7496 6577 7*
ISBN 0 7496 6583 1

The Little Red Hen
ISBN 0 7496 6578 5*
ISBN 0 7496 6585 8

The Nightingale
ISBN 0 7496 6579 3*
ISBN 0 7496 6586 6

Thumbelina
ISBN 0 7496 6580 7*
ISBN 0 7496 6587 4

RHYME TIME
Squeaky Clean
ISBN 0 7496 6588 2*
ISBN 0 7496 6805 9

Craig's Crocodile
ISBN 0 7496 6589 0*
ISBN 0 7496 6806 7

Felicity Floss: Tooth Fairy
ISBN 0 7496 6590 4*
ISBN 0 7496 6807 5

Captain Cool
ISBN 0 7496 6591 2*
ISBN 0 7496 6808 3

Monster Cake
ISBN 0 7496 6592 0*
ISBN 0 7496 6809 1

The Super Trolley Ride
ISBN 0 7496 6593 9*
ISBN 0 7496 6810 5

* hardback

Goldilocks and the Wolf

For Lynda and Charles

First published in 2008
by Wayland

Wayland
338 Euston Road
London NW1 3BH

Wayland Australia
Level 17/207 Kent Street
Sydney, NSW 2000

Series Editor: Louise John
Editor: Katie Powell
Cover design: Paul Cherrill
Design: D.R.ink
Consultant: Shirley Bickler

A CIP catalogue record for this book is available from the British Library.

ISBN 9780750255165

Printed in China

Wayland is a division of Hachette Children's Books,
an Hachette Livre UK Company

www.hachettelivre.co.uk

Goldilocks and the Wolf

Written by Hilary Robinson
Illustrated by Simona Sanfilippo

WAYLAND

Goldilocks ran from the Three Bears'
house, down into Bluebell Wood.

She stopped to rest beside a stream
and saw Little Red Riding Hood.

Goldilocks told her the story
of the bears she'd met that day.

Of how she'd tried their porridge...

...and why she'd run away.

Red Riding Hood said, "Are you feeling hungry? Would you like a bun?"

But as she laid the picnic cloth,
Goldilocks screamed, "Run!"

A wolf sat down between them
and said, "Buns! How kind of you!"

10

But the girls knew if they stayed there he'd try to eat THEM, too!

11

"Quick, run!" said Goldilocks again, and both girls turned quite pale.

12

They went to hide behind a hedge,
but they spied the wolf's brown tail!

13

They ran and hid beside the pond.

Then Goldilocks gave a cry!

For peeping over the top of the reeds was the wild wolf's winking eye!

"I know," said Goldilocks.
"Let's take cover here."

16

But, over by the gate, they saw
the wolf's brown pointed ear!

"Let's go!" they cried. "The riverbank has trees to hide beneath!"

18

But peeping through the rustling leaves
they saw the wolf's sharp teeth!

Goldilocks said, "Follow me!
We'll race towards that farm.

20

"We'll try and find the Three Bears there and raise the wolf alarm!"

"Listen," said Red Riding Hood, "I've got a good idea.

22

"Let's go to my Grandmother's house. She lives really very near."

But, as they ran, they heard a howl,
that echoed round the trees,
and when they turned around they saw
the wolf down on his knees.

"Don't go," he sobbed.
"Oh, please don't go.
Don't leave me all alone.

26

"No one wants to be my friend.
I'm always on my own!

"I'm just a friendly, gentle wolf.
I'm really very meek.

"And all I want to play with you
is a game of...

"...HIDE and SEEK!"

START READING is a series of highly enjoyable books for beginner readers. **The books have been carefully graded to match the Book Bands widely used in schools.** This enables readers to be sure they choose books that match their own reading ability.

Look out for the Band colour on the book in our Start Reading logo.

The Bands are:

Pink Band 1

Red Band 2

Yellow Band 3

Blue Band 4

Green Band 5

Orange Band 6

Turquoise Band 7

Purple Band 8

Gold Band 9

START READING books can be read independently or shared with an adult. They promote the enjoyment of reading through satisfying stories supported by fun illustrations.

Hilary Robinson loves jumbling up stories and seeing how they turn out. Her life is a jumbled up lot of fun, too! Hilary writes books for children and produces radio programmes for BBC Radio 2 and, because she loves doing both, she really does feel as if she is living happily ever after!

Simona Sanfilippo loves to draw and paint all kinds of animals and people. She enjoyed reading illustrated fairytales as a child, and hopes you will enjoy reading these fairytale jumbles, too!